B K

As

Written by: Ash Ericmore

Copyright © 2022 Ash Ericmore

ISBN: 9798804700318

CHAPTER 1

Grace scurried down the road. Fucking canvasing for the Green Party. How the fuck had she ended up there? Well, *Carol*, that was how. She'd fallen hook, line, and damned sinker for that woman. Down the pub. On a Friday night. Four years ago. Damn it. Was it really that long ago?

She turned up the path of the first house in Dalby Avenue. Long road. She looked back at the gate and wished she'd never started all this. A *sigh*. *Huff*. To the house. The garden path was long. She looked around for stickers in the windows or on the doors, hoping that there was one for the Conservatives or something.

That way she could turn back and not bother knocking.

But there was nothing. Shame. This road—the one before it, and probably the one after it—was a giant waste of time. These houses were *all* conservatives. Rich area. Pen pushers. Insurance brokers. Bankers. The usual. Rich, richer, poor, poorer. She knew that was hardly the attitude, but what the hell? At the front door she straightened down her clothes—a beige business suit thing. It had come from a charity shop and the *party* had paid for it for her. Well, it wasn't like she was going to wear her own clothes for this sort of thing, now, was she?

Big breath. *And knock*.

She hammered on the wooden part of the door. There was frosted glass that she could see through, and while she waited she did give a little look in. A bit of a nose, as it were. The front door was pretty worn. Unusual for such a good area. Absently, she let herself look up the front of the house. Three storey. A little tatty. Maybe she'd misjudged the road. Maybe there had been a downturn in the quality of living up there since she last walked the pavement, some years back.

Noticing a light behind the door—something within the house moving—she straightened herself again and waited.

The door opened. Guy behind it looked pretty rough. Like he was hung over. Just got up or something. She smiled her best smile and when he didn't say anything she asked, "Do you know who you're voting for yet?"

The man frowned. Deep lines inset into his forehead as his glasses slipped a little down his face. "What?"

"The by election," she said. *Smile*. Always smile. She tapped the green rosette on her lapel. "The Green Party, Mr. Dylan Rogers. Can he count on your support?"

The man continued to look at her like she was speaking German. "I don't know," he said.

He seemed confused. Maybe he had been drinking? Grace glanced at her watch. Seemed a bit early. She thrust a leaflet at him. "Please, do you have any questions that I can help you with, to help you make a more informed choice about your Green representative in the next election?" *Smile*.

He shook his head. "I work nights," he said.

That explained a lot.

Shit.

"Why don't you just fuck off?" he continued. Then he slammed the door.

It wasn't the first time she'd been told to fuck off

by a homeowner. Not in a street like this, though. She looked up at the house again. Well, a street like this *used* to be, apparently. She straightened her clothing again, turned on her heel and went back to the street. She had a clipboard under one arm and a bag with leaflets in slung over the other shoulder. She pulled a pen from the inside of her jacket and marked the house, 1, with the comment 'non-committal'. She then turned up the street walking towards the next house.

There was a short walk between paths. The houses were all detached and the gardens pretty large. It gave her time to think about what she was going to say to Carol. *Fuck off*, she was going to say. And *why this road*, and that, *he smelt*.

He hadn't smelt, but she would say he did. Make Carol feel bad. Carol didn't do this *street walking* bullshit. No. She had a desk at what they referred to as headquarters. It was an abandoned shop on the high street that the council said they could use for a song. Slap of green paint on the outside and some furniture from a company in the process of going out of business and a trash pile became *headquarters*.

Carol was going to have to buy her dinner for this.

Do something nice for her.

To her.

Hm.

Yes.

She opened the gate at the next house. This was more like it. From the path, the hedges looked overgrown, but that was by design, to try and make the place more private. Once within the walls, the house—previously hidden by the growth—was quite splendid. Looked like it might have been something else at some point. A doctor's office when the town was small, maybe a vets, converted into a private house for those rich—*conservative*—enough to afford it. There was ivy growing up the walls, and a gravel driveway that stopped at the main doors.

She walked up the path slow, taking her time, taking in the feeling of it being a public garden, something like a castle garden, before she got to the drive, and crossed. To the front door.

There was a bell.

An *actual* fucking bell on a rope. She pulled it, standing under the brick archway that protected the front door from the elements. It clanked. She heard it both inside and out. Regal, like. Turning, to face the gardens, Grace couldn't help but grin. Oh, what it would be like to live there, she pondered. A glance to the sky. It was drab. Rainy, but even just standing there, the clouds seemed whiter.

The door behind her opened and she turned. Almost forgot the patter she had down, faced with a gentleman, older in years, with a charming smile on his face. "Good morning," she said. "I'm with the Green Party."

C H A P T E R   2

The man stood and smiled at her. He was an older man. Striking white hair, and he was tall, slender, his build betrayed his age, of that she was sure. In his face he looked as old as the hills, and yet he didn't have so much of a glimmer of that hunch all older men get. He was taller than she was, looking down at her face, as she flustered slightly over the words she needed to get out. "I'm sorry," she said, keeping the smile painted on. "Where was I?"

"You're with the Green Party," the man said. He had a twinkle in his eyes. Like he was flirting. Teasing her. One or the other.

Far too old for that sort of malarkey, surely? "Yes," Grace said. "The Green Party. Have you decided how you're going to vote?" That came out wrong. It was all coming out wrong. Damn this fucking job. Maybe she should go and shelf stack instead? Maybe that was the way forward. *Fucking politics*.

As if he could sense her apprehension, see it in her face, his smile, warm, turned to a grin. "It's funny you should be passing," he said. "I could use a younger pair of eyes on something. Do you mind?" He stepped back away from the door slightly and gestured that she should enter the house.

Grace was unsure. The rule was that you never entered a house when canvassing, particularly alone, and she had only broken that rule once when she really needed to piss. That was a woman, elderly, too. She shouldn't. "I shouldn't," she said. "Rules." She felt the need to back up her decline with a statement that would belay this man's feelings, as he was clearly going to be offended should he feel that she wasn't entering because she was afraid.

"Oh, do come." His voice had a jovial edge to it. Stuck his head out into the garden. "There's no one looking," he said. Sly. Cheeky. *Playful.*

Grace's smile turned from the painted on one to the real one. She felt like she might be blushing. "Oh, go on," she said. Rebellious. Breaking the rules. Sneaking out the gates of school at lunch for a quick ciggie. She looked around, and slipped by him into the house. "What can I help with?"

The man closed the door. He turned the key. Locking it. Grace's eyes dropped as she watched, and he must have noticed. "Don't be alarmed," he said. "You can't be too careful." He indicated with his eyebrows to the side. "Had some ruffian types move in next door."

She understood that much. And he left the key in the lock. Waved her to follow him as he left the hallway and headed to the room on the left.

The house was big. It was archetypically the sort of house you'd see in a Hallmark romance … or a gothic horror. Tall spires on the outside, but nothing inside, just rounded bits of house made to look pretty. Georgian bar leading in the windows. Inside, the man had decorated in keeping with it too. It was all dark wood and reds. Golds. Framed pictures. Very expensive, Grace was sure, but certainly not to her taste. It made it look like a chintzy hotel in the middle of nowhere. She followed him through to the library.

The house was bigger than she thought.

There was a fire in the fireplace, a small one. She wondered if it was real, or if it was one of those gas real-effect ones. Around the walls were books with leather bound spines. Made it look like a lawyer's office from one of those American dramas. In the middle of the room was a reclining chair with a small table next to it.

Out of place, on the table, was a laptop.

"I've never understood that thing," he said, waving to it. "My children demand I have it and then get frustrated when I can't find the photos they claim they had stuck in an email. I'm beginning to think that they're not sending me anything and are trying to make me look like I've lost what few marbles I have left. Get their hands on their inheritance early." He looked around the ceiling of the room, like he was reminiscing. Then his look dropped to Grace. He laughed, looking at her look of horror. "No, no," he said. "Of course they're not. I'm only fussing. No. That's why I'd like you to take a look. I'm not built for these modern technologies. Barely understand my TV these days." He dropped his hand, open palmed to the chair, and positioned himself behind it, wanting her to sit.

Grace liked the old man. Sure. He seemed sweet. Innocent. Perhaps from a different time. But she was still wary. He wanted her to sit, where she couldn't see him. Him behind her. But equally, she looked at him. Yes, tall, but old. He was frail, surely. Her smile wavered.

"I'd just like you to show me how to see my granddaughter. They live up north now, and it's too far for me to travel, and they won't bring her to me for a few weeks, maybe months." His warmth looked fragile. He looked hurt.

"Of course," she said. "Let's see what we can do." Grace sat at the laptop. It was on the desktop. No email open. "What email do you use?"

"Here," he said. He pushed the laptop a little closer to her. "See what you can find." He started dawdling towards the door of the library. "Back in a moment."

Grace watched him go. Where was he going? Did he want her to just poke about in his computer while he wasn't looking? She looked at the screen. It looked like it had barely been touched since it had left the warehouse. She used Google for her email. Supposed a lot of people used that these days. She opened the browser, and waited for the screen to appear. Then she clicked on the link to open the email.

It asked for a password.

No password. She clicked in the box, hoping it would fill it itself, maybe had been told to remember it. No. The email address in the pre-filled box was *normangriggs*. She wondered if that was the old man. Made sense.

She looked around the room. Warm. It was too warm in there. Old person warm. She remembered her nan's living room was always hot when she was younger. The books all looked to be in some sort of order, well thumbed, too. Maybe he was a retired solicitor or something. Grace sat back. Looked at the space above the fireplace. There was fine edge around a darker patch of the wallpaper, the colours around it faded, like there should be something hung there. There was nothing. Probably should have been a portrait. Something like that.

Listening, she could still hear him, pottering around. Grace got up, she went to the door and listened again. He was in one of the other rooms. "Hello?" she called, unwilling to take a pot shot at his name. "Excuse me?" She looked at the front door.

Part of her just wanted to leave. She wasn't comfortable. He was nice enough. Of course. It wasn't him, it was her.

There was a clatter in the room off to the side of the stairs, and she walked to it. She glanced through.

The posh carpet underfoot had given to white tiles. The kitchen. A wooden table in the middle of the room with four chairs around it. Old fashioned, yet expensive looking kitchen furniture, cupboards, that sort of thing. He was hunched over the kettle, pushing teabags into cups. Fine china by the look of it.

"Excuse me?" she said again.

The man jumped. "Oh," he said, turning. "I didn't see you there." His look of surprise morphed once again to a warm smile. "Any luck with the wretched thing?"

Grace shook her head. "It needs a password," she said. "Do you have one?"

"Oh, yes. Of course. It's …" he paused, thinking, then continued, "old trafford, with a capital O and T, with no spaces."

Grace nodded and left the kitchen, back to the library. She sat at the computer and put the password in.

The email unlocked, and she glanced down the list. A lot of unopened emails. "What's your son's name?" she called, louder than she did before, knowing where he was.

"Nicky," he called back.

"Nicky," she echoed, looking at the list of senders. "Nicky," again, absently. Couldn't see his name, but that didn't mean a lot. She looked around the screen for the search box. Not used to this application, she tended to do everything on her phone these days.

The man appeared at the door. "Tea," he said. He was carrying a silver tray with two cups and saucers on. "It is the least I can do."

Grace smiled. It was the last thing she wanted. To be honest, she wanted to leave now, regardless. Time was ticking on and she'd get into trouble if she didn't get the whole road done that morning. "I'm into your email, but I don't see his name."

He was looking around awkwardly trying to find somewhere to put the tray. The only table being the one with the laptop on it, and that wasn't large enough to take the tray. Eventually he seemed to tire of the whole thing, and he put the tray to the floor. He was making *um* and *ah* noises like he didn't know what to say.

She'd flustered him and that made her feel bad. Sweet old man. "Did you have the painting taken down recently?" she asked, trying to distract him.

He stood, bolt upright and looked at her. Blankly. "Hm?"

She motioned to the gap over the fireplace. "There used to be a painting there, didn't there?"

He glanced to the wall, but returned his look to her immediately he knew what she was talking about. "How do you know there used to be a painting there?"

"The paper," she said. "It's faded." Her smile dropped a little. He seemed … annoyed.

"That's very astute of you. Yes. I had it taken down." He stared at the gap for a few seconds. Then started up again with some fire. "The child," he said. "It was a portrait, and I wanted …" another pause, like he was thinking, "… the child painted in."

"I didn't know you could do that."

"What?" he replied, almost snapping at her.

"Painting someone into a picture." Grace spoke with hesitation. It was definitely time for her to leave.

"I'm sorry," he said. He seemed to be trying to collect his thoughts. "I'm just little tired." He picked up a cup and saucer from the floor. "You must think me a terrible host." He handed it to her. "My name is Weston, and you are?"

"Grace," she said, instinctively taking the drink as he handed it to her.

"Of course you are." His smile returned.

C H A P T E R   3

Weston sipped from the second cup as he stood over Grace. "So you can't find a picture from my son?" he asked, swallowing back the hot liquid.

Grace rested her cup down on the small table. "No. What is his email address, maybe I can search for it?"

Weston leant forward, looking at the screen, but picked up Grace's cup and saucer and handed it back to her. Probably didn't want the drink on the table next to the laptop. She wasn't going to spill it. She wasn't stupid. But she understood his apprehension.

She took a sip. The tea tasted a bit shit. She had never been one for tea at the best of times, but this was dishwater quality. The sort of tea you got when you bought a bacon roll and a cuppa for a quid at some shit bakery. She placed the drink down by the side of the chair, and shot a quick smile to him. "His email?" she repeated.

"Oh," Weston shuffled to the side, sounding a little unsure of what he was supposed to be thinking. "Yes." Then came the familiar chink of china, as he shuffled into Grace's cup and saucer on the floor, tipping it over. "Oh, bugger," he said, shuffling backwards.

"No harm," Grace said. She was a people pleaser. She was down on her knees before she knew it, and dabbing at the liquid on the hardwood floor with a serviette from the tray. "I've got it."

"Yes," Weston replied. "Yes you have."

He sounded a little different, Grace thought, as

she mopped up the piss liquid.

Weston reached down next to her, retrieving the silver tray.

"Nearly there," she said.

Then Weston slammed the silver tray into the side of her head.

Grace wobbled, but didn't flop down unconscious to the floor or anything. She was stunned. It was going to take her time to process what Weston had just done. Maybe. *Why?* She was still on her knees, and her brain was screaming at her to get up. Get out. Flight. Flee. Run. *Why are you not moving motherfucker?* This chump just tried to take you down. Why are you in this house? What's going on?

Then he hit her again, grunting with the force he put in behind it.

This second blow didn't feel at hard as the first, although a lot of that could have been down to the weird numbness she had creeping across her head. She turned her head, slightly, just to look at him, still stood over her. As she did, spikes of pain leapt into her neck and shoulder, and just as sudden as he had hit her, she felt like she'd been hit by a car. She tried to speak. Her brain wanted her to scream. But nothing came out. Was that shock? She didn't know. She managed to drop the serviette, wet with insipid tea, and put her hand up, to the arm of the chair she'd been sat in. *Push yourself up*, the voice in her head was saying. *You were stupid*, yes, *but don't be stupid anymore.* He's a shuffling old man. You can get to the front door. The key is still in it. *Remember?*

She did remember. The key *was* in the front door. She tried to glance to the door of the library, get her bearings, but her head didn't seem to want to do that. It wanted to roll around like she was drunk. She hadn't been drinking … it was too early for that. Weston lifted his leg up. She thought that he was moving surprisingly spryly for someone his age, or that perhaps she had misjudged him. He kicked her.

The flat of his foot landing hard on her left breast. The pain from that shot through her body, and took the wind from her. She fell back, crashing into the chair, pushing it aside, and slumping to the floor.

Get up. The voice was adamant. *Get up now, before it's too late.*

But she feared it already was. The pain from the kick shuddered through her body. It had caught her completely off guard, and she couldn't seem to shake the dumbness in her head. Weston was standing next to her, as she flopped from side to side trying to get a grip on her bodily movement, when she noticed he still had the tray in his hand. There was a smear of something across it. It looked deep in colour. Hard to tell what it was, being on the polished silver. Odd that someone who owned polished silver couldn't make a decent cup of tea.

She looked at the cup and saucers, bone china, broken on the floor of the library. Weston making no move to clean it up. It would stain. She rocked over onto her back, blind in one eye. She rubbed at it. Why had she gone blind all of a sudden? Then she looked at the back of her hand. Blood. She had blood in her eye. She tried to blink it away but that just seemed to make it worse. She did manage to get the word, "No," out, and then, "Please," but Weston didn't seem to be listening.

He was looking down at her, grinning. He seemed to be taking some great delight in this. Whatever *this* was. He was going to kill her, wasn't he? Why? What had she done? What could she have done different?

There was a ring of black around her sight, drawing in, closer to the centre. Taking what little she could see out of the one eye, as he stood and watched. She let the muscles in her neck relax, the pain stabbing at her as she tried to keep it held up, and why? Just to look at him, looking at her. She felt the floor behind her as her head bounced a couple of times. It felt like her head was full of liquid. Slopping about in there. A spark of fire on the side of her head. From where he'd hit her with the tray. The first time. The warmth of her blood on her skin. Torso suffering from the stress of the kick.

Blackness, coming from all directions.

Why?

CHAPTER 4

The black parted briefly for the light to come. Grace closed her eyes again, after trying to open them. Shit. She felt … rough. Sick. There was a strange queasiness in her gut. One that was creeping up to her head like a hangover, but not. Something. Else. She rolled. She was laying down. On something coarse.

Moving made her head feel worse. She tried to open her eyes again. The light, bright. She closed them, remembering Weston. Remembering what had happened. Her eyes snapped open, the light be damned. Looked around. She was laying on a low bed. One of those old foldup beds that you got out the attic when your teenager had a friend over to sleep. Too old to share. Too young to get shitfaced and black out on the sofa.

The room. It had no windows. There was a corner. The room, not square, with part of the room out of her line of sight. L-shaped. She brought her eyes to a squint. The pain was hard. Heavy. Made her tired. He'd hit her with something metal. She might be concussed. Remembering her blood in the eyes she reached up and touched her face. Nothing there. No dried blood. Nothing. Her fingers started to tenderly feel around her head. She hissed air in, as she found a lump, hair wound together, and felt signs of a gash on her. Bad one. It stung. Made her headache throb worse. Felt like someone was stabbing at her. An ice pick. Straight in the brain.

It felt like her eyes were bulging.

Like there was too much blood in her brain. She

breathed slowly. Eyes shut. Trying to get her bearings. She'd taken a beating. Didn't know how long she'd been unconscious. Didn't know where she was. Her mouth was dry as a fucking desert. Grace tried to move again. Aches. Bumps. Bruises. There seemed to be something wrong with every inch of her. And she felt tired.

She was going to sit up. Look around.

Swift motion. It was for the best. She swung her legs from the bed, and pulled herself up to sit. Eyes still closed. The blood in her head sloshed from side to side as she waited for it to all go away. She wanted to puke. Well, she didn't want to, but her body wanted to eject whatever was in her. Out onto the floor. But she had no intention of allowing that. She was holding it in. Wait. Wait until she had more information.

She cracked her eyes open again. No windows. Glance up. There was a bare bulb in the middle of the ceiling on this half or the room. Bare bricks. It was cold. Not breezy cold, but cold like a fridge. She slipped her arms around herself. Her jacket had been taken from her. She was still wearing the thin shirt from beneath it. She touched down her body. The rest of her clothes still present. Her shoes were gone though. Her gut had settled a little. She opened her eyes more. Enough to see the rest of the room. The brick walls. Painted white. They were dirty. Cobwebs hung, looking like they'd been there for years. Like she was in a shed or something. The floor, bare laid concrete.

There was no door. Not that she could see. It must be around the corner. She took a deep breath and prepared herself to stand. Rolled her shoulders. She felt like she'd been pushed down a flight of stairs. That, and the sickness. She didn't want to stand and black out. She wanted to get out. From wherever the fuck she was. She needed to get out. People would miss her soon enough, but they wouldn't know where she was.

But … but, it would be okay. She would remain calm and rational. Probably all a mistake. She'd just get up. Leave.

She knew the thoughts were ridiculous, but it was all she had right then. She moved her feet forward, placed her hands on the bed, and got ready to push. Then she noticed. Something on her ankle. She hadn't seen it before, hadn't felt it. Hadn't … "Hello?" she called. The sound of her own voice. It sounded like she was underwater. She moved her jaw from side to side. Her mouth felt fine apart from the dryness. The thing on her ankle. A shackle. She was chained to something. She moved her foot and the chain moved. She could hear only the dullest of sounds from it. That was why she hadn't heard it. She reached down and grabbed it, tugged on it.

It made the puke in her gut bolt towards her mouth. She quickly sat back up as the room started to spin. It calmed the sickness, pushing it back down, but made the thickness in her head throb. Fuck. "Hello?" She knew that she was calling weakly. Not by sound, but just feel. "Hello?" She pulled her leg to the side, trying not to make herself feel worse, and not wanting to bend over. Following the chain, she found she was shackled to the bed frame. A ring of metal with a padlock on her leg, and the bed. She blinked the tears back.

What had happened? Why? Shit. Fuck. She needed to call Carol. *Carol*. Grace ignored the sickness and looked around. Patting herself down.

Her handbag was gone. Jacket. Gone. There was a small bedside table. On it were two pills. A glass of water. She frowned at it. She wanted the water so much. So, so much. But fuck was she touching it. The pills? Pain killers? Fucking arsenic?

She couldn't hold the tears back. She could feel them streaming down her face. She wiped the back of her arm over it. Left smudges of makeup on the arm of her shirt. She was cold. Scared.

Someone had kidnapped her.

CHAPTER 5

It felt like hours. She tried to lay. Sit. She yanked on the chain. Nothing. There was nothing she could do, no way to get more than a couple of feet from the bed. Couldn't see around the corner. No way of knowing the time. Couldn't see the door.

All she heard was the buzz of the electricity zipping through the light that hung from the ceiling. Her own breathing.

Then, eventually, she heard footsteps. Above her. *Through* the ceiling. She followed the sound. Cutting from left to right, and dropping away in the distance. For the first time she concentrated on the ceiling. It looked like it was floor boards. Hard to tell, being dark up there, and all. The bulb in the room, it gave off so little illumination that she couldn't really tell what *was* up there.

She noticed dust falling in the air, hovering in the dim light. So the ceiling couldn't be plastered. Maybe she was in the basement of Weston's house? She shook her head, tenderly. It still hurt like a motherfucker. Pain across her shoulders. Stabbing pains she'd never felt before, bruises, scrapes. She knew that under her clothes she must be black and blue, beaten to crap, but she wasn't about to start peeling her clothes back to examine herself. There might be cameras in the room. In the darkness. She'd seen films. Films about stupid, thoughtless, women going into homes of men and never coming out. She'd joked about it with Carol. *Who'd be that stupid, right?*

Yeah. Who'd be that stupid.

Her shoulders slumped. If it was lunchtime then they might miss her back at headquarters. Maybe. If they weren't too busy. Carol got tied up in all sorts of shit, and half the time Grace didn't know if it mattered if she was even there or not.

Surely, someone would notice she was missing? What if it was later than that? What if it was the evening? Had the police been called? Was there someone looking for her? What if Carol came to this same house and started asking difficult questions?

She realised she'd began sobbing. Quietly. Then she screamed out. Loud. She sounded like she was in pain, hurt, maybe fallen, but that wasn't it. It was anguish. She was distraught. And helpless.

And she didn't like being helpless.

Still, the scream seemed to draw someone upstairs into motion, as the footsteps begun again and there were new sounds. Doors. Latches. Locks. Then the sound of a door opening. Around the corner, where she couldn't see.

"Hello?" she called out, tentatively. Before realising that was the sort of shit that happened in horror films and quite regularly got people killed. Fuck it. She was behaving like one of the body count. *Pull it together, woman.* "Help," she shouted at the top of her voice. "Help me, I'm chained up in here."

"There's no one to hear you, and no one is coming." The voice came from around the corner. Weston. She could tell immediately.

She was still sobbing and his words burst her bubble as far as shouting went. So she just sobbed more.

"I'm sorry about all that, but I had to restrain you somehow, and you wouldn't just drink the tea, would you? No. You were all questions. Difficult questions. And look where it got you."

He came around the corner. She would have lunged at him, but having already established that she could barely make it two feet from the bed, she didn't see the point. She'd only hurt her ankle. And she guessed that she was going to need all the strength she could muster. He was carrying that fucking silver tray. She knew it was the same one, as it was slightly warped. From her fucking head. She stayed on the bed, and drew her feet up, backing herself against the cold white painted wall behind her. Her knees up under her chin. Arms wrapped around them. "What do you want?" she asked. "Who are you?"

Weston put the tray down on the floor and shoved it close enough to her that she would be able to reach it when she got from the bed. He glanced to the small table. "You haven't taken the paracetamol." He sighed. "Or drunk the water." There was a tinge of disappointment in his voice.

"So you can poison me?" she snapped.

Weston shook his head. "My dear, if I was going to do that, I would have hardly gone to the trouble of dragging you down here in the first place, now would I?" He waved his hand at her like a forgetful professor. "And on that, sorry about your back and shoulders and such. You somewhat thumped down the stairs."

He did have a point. Grace glanced to the painkillers. The water. She knew that part of her headache might well be dehydration.

"I brought you something to eat," he said. He gestured to the tray, now on the floor.

She couldn't see it, and wasn't about to take her eyes from him, let alone get down on the floor in front of him. He was smiling at her.

"As you will," he said. "You'll change your mind eventually." Then he turned and disappeared back around the corner.

Grace heard the door go, open, then close. "Wait," she called, but it was too late. She scooted to the edge of the bed and looked the *food* he'd left. A paper plate. No cutlery. Bread. Buttered. Looked like a lump of cheese. Where did he get off thinking she was going to eat anything?

She could feel the pain in her stomach. Knew that she was hungry, but fuck him, and fuck this. She started to pull on the chain again. The end attached to the bed was wrapped securely around the metal bed frame and the bed was bolted to the floor. It looked like a pre-prepared prison. Somewhere that Josef Fritzl would have in *his* basement. She looked down at herself. She was cold. Hungry.

Then to the pills. *Paracetamol*, he'd said. What if they were something else? Something he wanted to get her hooked on? Shit. She looked between the food and the pills.

In for a penny.

C H A P T E R   6

Grace rolled the pills in her fingers. They looked like standard out of the packet paracetamol. The liquid smelt of nothing. It looked like water. She brought the glass to her lips, touching the fluid on her dried, chapping skin. It felt like water. It had that taste, that feel of water that had been there sometime. Which it may have been. She thought. Hours. She'd been awake for what must be hours. God only knew how long she had been unconscious. Fuck it. She took a small swig of the water. Rolled it in her mouth. Tasted like water. Must be water. She swallowed it, putting the glass back down on the side table. Then she waited. She waited to see if she was going to black out, or worse. Maybe start convulsing. Maybe a burning pain in her gut where whatever it was started to burn through her stomach lining.

But nothing came.

She realised she was counting in her head. In seconds. Timing how long the water—yes, that was what she was calling it—had been inside her. She reached two minutes and when nothing had happened, she picked the glass back up and took a chug. Half the glass down in one. It felt good. Refreshing. She was able to move her tongue about in her mouth without it feeling like she'd somehow gotten sand in there. She licked the dryness from her lips, rubbing them over her teeth to scrape away the dried crust that had formed, and then swallowing that back. A taste of blood in there somewhere.

Grace raised her hand to touch her head again,

and thought better of it. She wasn't dead. She wasn't bleeding anymore. At least that probably meant that she wasn't going to die from the head wound.

She wished she had a mirror. So she could see what she looked like. What damage she had. Tenderly poking at her face didn't get her anywhere. It all just hurt. Fucker had fucked her up proper, hadn't he? Well. Wait until the police came. She looked at the pills, still in her hand, the water in the other. Had to have been five minutes since she drank it. She'd stopped counting. Why would there be anything wrong with the pills?

But why would he be trying to make her feel better?

Fuck. She took some more of the water into her mouth, and then slipped the pills in. Swallowed them back with ease. Then she put the water down on the table. She wanted to drink it so badly. Every fibre in her being wanted to. But she didn't know if he might not come back. He might be gone for hours. Maybe until tomorrow. Maybe he'd never return.

Her heart sunk the more she thought about it. She was trapped down there. No one knew where she was. The only person who had actually seen her in that road was that miserable fucker next door. He was the only witness that she'd even *gotten* to the that street, and was he going to say anything if the police came knocking? Was he even going to remember?

She was weeping again.

She tried to stop herself. She could feel that she was dehydrated. Wasting the water. It was better off inside her. She let a sigh out. What the fuck did she know? Were tears even water? Making her feel worse, her stomach gripped, and twisted. *The pills were poison, weren't they?* she thought. As she sat there, knees on the bed. She breathed deeply, calmed, and the twisting in her gut stopped. *Fear*. It was just fear.

Maybe the painkillers were just that.

But why?

She wasn't paying enough attention, and hadn't heard Weston until he opened the door around the corner. No footsteps. Nothing. He came to the corner and looked at her. He was staring at her when she looked up at him. He was pissed. His gaze moved from her to the tray on the floor. The water. Back to her.

He stamped across the small space, treading on the tray, scattering the bread to the floor.

Fear gripped her tightly and Grace shimmied back across the bed, trying to get herself as far away from him as she could, but he was on her. He threw punches into her. Randomly. He didn't seem to care where they landed. It was just a torrent of blows, angry, violent. He was grunting with the excursion, over her. Hot. She could feel him. His body, his presence. The blows numbing her at first.

Then she started to feel it. Probably the adrenaline, the fear, washing off. She felt a jab, hard in her ribs. It felt like a horse had kicked her. Then another, on her arm. She remembered being punched in the top of the arm at school like that, as her arm numbed.

Grace tried to curl into a ball, covering her head, bringing her knees up into her chest, trying so desperately to protected herself. He used one hand to pull her arm away from her. Their eyes able to meet. He punched her, tight fisted, brutally, into the side of the head. The pain screamed out. She felt blood let from the tray wound, re-opened. She tried to scream, but she couldn't, her throat was tight. *It wouldn't let her scream.*

She had tears on her face. She couldn't move. Couldn't run—the chain saw to that—but she couldn't fight back either. *You have to stop him*, the voice in her head was saying as it bounced from side to side like she was on a train, rocking.

A blow to her chest. On her breast, the pain blossoming out, fire burning across her. "Please," she said. The only word she managed to get out.

And he stopped.

He let her go. Huffing. Standing at the side of the bed over her. She could see him, red faced. His skin rolled in wrinkles where he was ravaged by anger.

Grace lowered her hands from her face. She could feel the wet heat of blood on her. The skin on her face was tightening where he'd bruised her, flesh swelling. Blood in her mouth. "Please," she said again, quietly. As loud as she could. Her chest burning with pain, her lungs tight, unable to get the air they desired into them. She felt like she'd run a marathon, and been driven over by a combine harvester, all at the same time.

Her left eye was closing. She wasn't closing it. Distension.

It made her tired. So tired. Her muscles so taut, they hurt. The blows, from where she hadn't felt them, rising pain. Her legs, arm, torso. Even on her back.

They still hadn't broken eye contact. Weston's colour was returning to normal as he pulled air into him. Then huffed it back out.

He relaxed his fist and then roughly took both her wrists in one hand. Binding them together with such strength he may as well have slapped cuffs on her.

Strength she didn't think a man of his years could have. Then he back-handed slapped her. She spat blood out, onto the sheet on the bed. She felt her nose close to air. Blood rushing down her face.

He released her, and Grace slumped to the bed. One eye closed, the other swollen shut. There was a ringing in her ears, and she could hear nothing again.

Good. The voice in her head. It was telling her to relax. There was nothing more to do. It sounded like it had given up.

CHAPTER 7

When Grace opened her eye, Weston was gone. She didn't know how long she'd laid there. Maybe she'd blacked out, maybe she'd fallen into a sleep. She had no idea, but she felt like she'd been unconscious. She was cold. She hurt. Everything hurt. She could hear herself breathing. That was something. It was an external sound. So he hadn't beaten the hearing from her. She reached up and touched her eye. It felt bulbous. It didn't hurt to touch as much as it hurt to move her arm to touch it.

She craned her head to look at her arm. Purple and red blotches adorned the skin. She touched her breast, bruised, and painful, and when she looked down at herself, her clothing was a ruin of blood.

Had to all be hers. It wasn't there earlier.

She looked at the sheets on the bed. Bloody too. Then she remember he'd wrecked her nose. She tried to sniff, but couldn't on one side. It was full of blood. She poked at it, and felt with the tip of her fingers. It was hard crusted. She must have been out of it for some time. There was a ridge on her nose that wasn't there before. She could see it. He'd fucked her up good.

Grace moved across the bed to the edge and looked at the floor. The tray was gone. The paper plate. The only thing that remained was the bread. Stood on. Trodden into the dirt. She went to reach for the water.

Gone.

"Please," she muttered. It was instinctual. She

wasn't talking to anyone in particular. She just wanted help. Any help. From anywhere. She just needed … something. The voice, it was saying that *she needed to escape*. This man, Weston, whatever his name really was, he was *fucking crazy*. He was going to *kill her*. Was she even listening?

She was. But she was also paralysed with fear. She wasn't built for this sort of thing. She was a nobody. She just wanted to live her life.

They're quitting words, the voice said. *You have to fight*.

Grace drew in a deep breath. When her chest started to move as the air got in, it started to hurt, tight, and bruised from the barrage of punches. *He was angry*, she thought. Because she hadn't taken his food. Gifts, maybe? The voice was right. She had to get out of this somehow. She looked at the bread on the floor, and the empty table.

Nothing left to do but wait.

She sat back on the bed, and wrapped her arms around herself. Cold. Must be the basement. It wasn't that cold … when? Yesterday? This morning? Fuck.

She listened to the movement above her again. Him, no doubt. There was clearly no one else in the house, that, or he wasn't worried about them knowing she was there. She didn't make a lot of noise when he beat her, but some. It didn't concern him. He came across the top of her. Then a few seconds later the door opened.

He came from behind the corner. Glanced around her.

She noticed he checked the chain. Making sure everything was in its place, no doubt.

"You won't get anything new, until you've had what you're given."

What the fuck did that mean?

Then he turned. Left her sight as he headed back towards the door.

"Wait," she said. She heard him stop walking, but he didn't come back. Wait? What for? *Bargain*, the voice said. *Tell him anything.* "What do you want?" she asked. "You can … have it." *Good.*

Then the sound of his footfalls began again, and the door closed. She listened to him cross the ceiling above her.

"Damn," she muttered.

Grace got off the bed. The floor was grimy. It looked black with something. Greasy shit. The sort of floor a workshop would have. She got down to her hands, and arched herself outwards, like a crab, so she didn't have to kneel to try and get her head closer to the corner. She wanted to see around. She wanted to know what was there. And she was safe, as long as she could hear him coming.

But it hurt.

Aches. Pains. Bruising. Swelling. Her years of yoga proving no use now, as she had never realised that she was supposed to do it while her instructor hit her repeatedly with a cricket bat. She spidered on the floor. Didn't want to put her knees down. She would cover herself in shit, *and then he'd know*.

She pulled the chain taut, as she crawled along the wall. Spidering to a stop, her head, eyes, mere inches from the corner of the wall. Unable to see. "Fuck," she muttered.

She crawled back to the bed and got to her feet. Pulled the single blood crusted sheet from the bed, and wrapped it around herself. The blood—*her* blood—had soaked through to the mattress below. She curled up on it. Pulled the sheet tight around her.

Tried to get warm.

C H A P T E R   8

Grace was awoken by the sound of the door unlocking. *Stupid*, the voice said. *Careless*. She moved to sit, wracked by pain, from every corner of her body. But she got up. The blood in her head sloshing around like she'd been down for hours. Maybe she had.

She blinked away the darkness, aware that there was the smallest amount of light coming in her left eye. That was something. Perhaps the swelling was going down? What did she know? She'd never gotten a black eye in her life. She'd never gotten into so much as a fight before.

Weston came to the corner. He looked at her. Grunted. "You still have food, I see."

She blinked at him. Looked to the side table. Nothing. There was no food. "What?" she said. It came out gnarly. She'd had nothing to drink in fuck knows how long. "What food?"

He pointed. To the ground between himself and the bed.

Grace leant forward. The bread. On the floor. Stood in. Caked in shit, and black stuff. She looked back to him. Frowning. "That's not food," she said. She knew that she shouldn't have said anything as soon as she had, but the words just slipped from her.

Weston didn't say anything. He just turned. Left.

She listened to him close the door. He didn't slam it. He just closed it. Then a short period of quiet, then the sound of him walking about upstairs.

She looked at the bread on the floor. There was

no way she could eat it. She hadn't even thought about food. Not thought about how hungry she was. Suddenly aware though, through the pain that pulsed around her body, her stomach started to growl. That was all she needed. She looked longingly at the side table, wishing there was water there. She knew that without water she would die quickly.

That wasn't what he wanted, though, was it? If he had wanted her dead, then surely she already would be?

She looked at the 'food' and sat back. She couldn't eat that. Disgusting.

The voice had fallen quiet. She knew it—the voice—was her. She knew it was one in her head, and that it was just her reasoning with herself, but she missed it when it was quiet.

The sound of Weston moving about again kept her eyes to the ceiling. She watched as he went back and forth a couple of times. It was the most she'd heard him move about without coming down to see her. She wondered what he was doing. He seemed to go AWOL for a few minutes, then he was crossing the floor again. Then quiet.

Then the door opened.

She sat there, swaddled in the sheet.

Weston came around the corner. He was holding a bowl. A silver dish like a cereal bowl. He came to her. Not worrying that he'd gotten within her circle, and he placed the bowl down on the mattress. "Eat," he said.

Grace looked at the bowl. It had shit in it. Faeces. The smell wafted up under her nose. She looked at it, wet … fresh. Her eyes jumped up to Weston. Was it … his? She shook her head. "What?" she said.

"Eat it," he said. He was calm. She could feel the

anger beneath the veneer, though. She could see he was boiling under there.

But she wouldn't do that. She'd rather eat the bread from the floor. "I-I can't," she said. She scooted slightly forward towards the edge of the bed. She looked, and went to reach forward. Take the bread from the floor and put that in her mouth. She'd appease him that way.

Weston moved his booted foot to the bread, and stomped down on top of it, covering it with his foot and winding it around, grinding it into the dirt. "Too late for that." He drew Grace's eyes to his, then he looked to the bowl of shit. "*That*," he said.

Grace shook her head. "I can't," she whispered. "Please."

"You keep saying that. Eat it now, while I watch, or I'll feed it to you."

She could sense the menace under his voice. Sinister. She looked at the bowl, but didn't move. What if he meant it? What if he was going to make her? Couldn't be. He was just angry that she hadn't eaten the bread.

The smell filled the air now. She could see the gelatinous brown goo wobble as she moved on the mattress. "Please," she said, again.

That seemed to tip the boat, and Weston suddenly moved. He reached down and slipped his fingers into the shit, scooping out a handful, and with his other hand he grabbed Grace by the hair. So fast, she was unable to do anything about it, her arms a tangle in the sheet, he pulled her head back and slapped his fingers scooped with shit to her lips.

She wanted to keep her mouth shut. It was what she wanted most in the whole world, but the instinct to scream was great, and she screamed. Her mouth open, he pushed the shit into her mouth, violating her with his fingers as he jammed them in, sloping shit between her lips. She was unable to clamp her teeth down. *Bite*, the voice was saying, *bite!* But he was knuckle deep into her maw, the stink of shit up her nose, she could taste it on her tongue. He pulled his hand out, reaching for another scoop, and Grace retched. She didn't mean to, but she retched and swallowed, his shit, warm shit, slipping down her throat like mucus being swallowed back.

The vile stuff, meeting the puke as it rose in her gullet, the two fetid things smooshing together.

Weston kept his hand from her mouth as she puked shit and vomit up, out, drooling more than firing, onto her face and clothes. Over the sheets. "Disgusting," he said. "So you really don't want to eat?" he barked, getting another scoop of faecal matter from the bowl, jamming it crudely into her mouth.

Grace nearly blacked out. The vomit rising took her breath as she tried so hard to fight, every inch of her being burning with pain from the previous onslaught. She tried to speak. She *tried* to push him away, but in the end she could do nothing against his strength, the attack so unexpected. She could feel tears, but after a couple of moments, that was all she *could* feel. The smell of the shit raided her nose, and her senses were taken one by one, until she just stopped and let him push it into her mouth.

With no control over her body, puke coming up, her mouth forced open by Weston, she just slumped, barely holding consciousness, her eyes shut.

The voice in her head was gone, replaced with a high pitched buzzing sound, and she wondered if this was the last thing she was going to hear … before death.

CHAPTER 9

Grace opened her eyes, suddenly. She awoke startled as if from a nightmare, but without the memory of it. She was laying on the bed. She could smell shit. It was all she could smell, and it just being there assaulted her.

Immediately she started to retch again.

She rolled, over the bed, instinctively, off the bed, and down to the floor, landing on her hands and knees. Face down, gasping for air like a diver resurfacing. Clear liquid escaped her mouth, running from her gut. She looked at it splattered on the floor beneath her. Breathing. Waiting.

She was confused.

Grace got to her knees, looking around the room. Everything was as it was before, except the bread on the floor was gone. There was water on the side table. She looked down at herself. She was smeared in a mash of blacks and browns, dried blood and human filth. She could still taste it. Hard to distinguish between the smell which was so fucking strong, and the taste, she realised there was dried shit in her mouth. She picked up the glass of water without thinking and drank it.

She got to the very end before realising what she had done. That was probably a day's water. She should have rinsed her mouth first, not swallowed. Shit.

Shit.

She put the glass back on the side, no more than half an inch of the liquid remaining. Got to her feet. Her back hurt. Jaw. Head. Pretty much everything …

still. She sat on the bed. The sheet was gone. He'd taken it. There was movement above her. She ignored it. Looked at the mattress, stained.

If you don't get away, the voice said, *you'll die*.

She nodded. It was true. She needed to get out the chain. Looking down at it, clasped to her ankle. She'd seen films. These things didn't come off—not without a key, or a hacksaw to … she looked away. Daren't even think about it.

The door around the corner opened. "Morning," came Weston's voice.

He came to the corner. Carrying a tray. Not the silver one. Plastic by the looks of it. He rested it down on the floor, said, "Back in a sec," and turned back. She heard him leave the room, but he never closed the door.

Grace looked at the tray. Bread and cheese. Paper plate. Pills. A pile of clothing, maybe. Cloths, rags? Too far away and in such a half-light it was hard to tell.

Weston returned. He was carrying a folding chair. He unfolded it on the far side of the room and set it down. He sat, wobbled himself to make sure the chair was sitting flat. When he was sitting, he was mostly out the light. She could see his shape, but not his face. She couldn't see what he was thinking.

"Food first, or clothes?" He paused. He was actually waiting for the answer.

Grace looked at the tray. She wanted the smell to go away. The stains on her. She felt gross, sticky. The voice said, *take the clothes. Retake your humanity*. It was right. It was always right. She felt like she wasn't acting human anymore. "The clothes," she said. She looked into the shadows where his face was. Couldn't judge anything from it. "Please," she added.

He stood. Went to the tray and picked up the pile of clothes, leaving some items behind, underneath. He tossed them to the bed, so that he didn't have to get close to her. Afraid, perhaps, that she might grab at him. She wouldn't have, of course. She was far too afraid. Broken. Beaten. "I brought you a clean sheet, too," he gestured to the sheet, folded on the tray. Out of reach. "And these." He took the box from the tray and tossed it to the bed.

She glanced at it. Wet wipes.

Grace gently placed her hand on the clothing, gently caressing the clean fabric. She then realised that her hands were clean. She looked at them. Almost spotless. She reached up and gently touched her face slipping her fingers around the bumps and lacerations that protruded from her. But there was no dried … anything … there. She glanced to him. He was stood in the light and she could see his face. He was gently smiling.

While she was out, he'd cleaned her face and her hands. And he was waiting for gratitude. That was why he was standing there. Now. *Right fucking now.*

Say it, said the voice.

"Thank you." She spoke so quietly that she could barely be heard, even in the silence of the room.

Weston returned to the chair. Sat. "Now strip," he said.

C H A P T E R   1 0

She looked at him, the words echoing around in her head. It all made sense suddenly. Why she was there. What he wanted. Her body. That was it. She looked down herself, sat on the bed, covered in blood, shit, vomit. She realised she'd started shaking harder. Harder than just from the cold. "What?" The word dropped out of her like a stone, mumbled. A subconscious attempt to stall. Buy time. To think.

"You heard me," he said. He voice was low, controlled. Sinister, but even.

Grace panicked, and with that panic, she started to undo the buttons on her shirt. She wasn't in any way attempting to do it *sexily*, but she was doing it slowly, if only because she was struggling to get her fingers to do what she wanted them to. Numb. Her whole body.

"Stand up," he said.

Grace did as he instructed. The voice inside her goaded her forward. *Do as he says. You've seen how violent he can be.* So she stood and unbuttoned her shirt, pulling from her. The material was stuck to her skin, a mixture of blood, snot, pus even, dried out on it. She pulled it off. Held it there, in front of her. A protective shield. Against him. Against his eye.

"Over there." He pointed to the corner, in the darkness, the far side of the tray.

Grace didn't want to drop the shirt. She knew that as soon as she did, she would need to start using her hands again. Remove another article of clothing. "Please," she whispered. She didn't even know if he heard her.

"There." His voice amped slightly.

She heard the displeasure there. Tossed the shirt over the tray and to the floor. She covered her body with her arms. They didn't cover much, but her torso was bare, but for her bra. Her skirt clinging to her. Her purity was there. Out. For him.

"Continue," he said.

There was anger in there now. She pulled her skirt open and let it drop to the floor. There was a smell. It came from her. She stood. Stockings. Bra. Knickers. Nothing else. She could feel the abrasion of her knickers on her skin. She'd pissed herself. When he'd been beating her, maybe. Hadn't felt it. Dried on her. When she was unconscious, she guessed. Her stomach broke the silence. A light, unconscious growl. Hunger pain stabbed at her. She just about felt it through all the other pain.

"More. All of it."

Grace nodded. She perched on the edge of the bed and took her stockings down her legs. Quickly. She was aware of how this probably looked to him, and she sure as shit didn't want to help him get off by playing into his fucking fantasy. She tossed them to the shirt. Picked up the skirt at the same time, and threw that across the room to the pile. She stood and dropped her panties, throwing them to the pile, and then her bra. She stood, naked, shivering in the cold. One arm over her breasts. The other hand in front of her mound. Her teeth chattering lightly. Getting colder by the second.

She couldn't see much of him. Not in the shadow. But he was sitting there watching her. Unmoving.

"Wash."

She looked at the wet wipes. Sure, she wanted to

wash. But she wanted him to fuck off, first. "Can I have some privacy?" she asked. Quietly. She didn't want to piss him off.

"No."

No questions. No arguments. No. *Just do it. Quickly. Get it over with.* She heard the voice and acted. Picked up the wet wipes and started to run them over her flesh. Sliding them through the sticky patches. Scrubbing the stains of blood from her pale skin. *He's going to want to fuck you when you're clean.* The voice was right, of course. Why else would any of this be happening? She tossed each wipe to the pile when she'd used it, moving onto the next. Before she'd finished the third one, he spoke.

"Dress," he said.

Grace didn't need telling twice. She hunched down and picked up the clothing he'd brought. A wavy fucking skirt and t-shirt. Still. It was clothing, not rape. She pulled the t-shirt on first, and then the skirt. By the time she stood, turning back to face him, he was up. In the light again. He'd gathered her dirty clothing and such into his arm. He took the paper plate with the bread and cheese from it, placing it on the floor, carefully. Took the tray. He stopped, at the corner of the room, and looked back at her. "Eat." Then he turned and left her sight, and the room. Closing the door quietly behind him.

She picked up the plate. The water from the side table. Pain killers. She took those first. Then she scoffed the food. It hurt to chew the bread. It was fresh enough, but her face hurt. Her jaw. She didn't care if he was poisoning her now, either. Although it appeared he had another agenda. She just didn't know what it was. Not sex. Not now, anyway.

She hated what she was wearing. Drank the

water. She closed her eyes. How long had she been down there? This was the first food she'd had. A day? Maybe a little longer. The police *had* to be looking for her by now.

CHAPTER 11

After finishing the food, she sat there, on the bed, her back against the wall. The clothing he'd brought was white. Wouldn't stay that colour for long. Not down there. There was something slopping around in her gut. She needed to use a bathroom. And not to piss. Not being able to see outside—not knowing if it was day or night—was throwing her all out of whack.

She'd taken the pills. Hopefully she could stay awake until he returned. The only way she could see out of this was to talk to him. The pain in her body, arms, face, then the food, and the painkillers … it all made her woozy. She was fighting to stay awake.

Then she heard him walk across the floor above her. He was coming back.

Grace rubbed her eyes with the back of her hands. She could still taste shit in her mouth, even after the water and the food. She rolled her tongue around her teeth and gums. She had to try and negotiate with him. Needed to look her best.

She was confused by him making her strip and not acting on it. Maybe he wasn't looking for that. But then why watch?

The door opened, and Grace slid to the edge of the bed. Sitting with her knees together and to the side. Trying to look … nice … for Weston. *Cunt.* He came around the corner. Looked a little surprised finding her sitting there like that. He looked her up and down like some rich twat might, his trophy wife ready to go out for the evening to a bank do. Then he looked to the empty plate. Glass. The pills gone. He nodded with some weird look of appreciation. "Good," he said.

Not much of a talker.

"Please," she said. "I need to use the bathroom." Grace held her lower stomach to try and underline it.

Weston nodded, loading his tray back up with things to remove.

More, said the voice. "Please," she said again. "I'll do anything you want."

Weston stopped, mid stoop to the plate. Still on the bed. He was close to her. Close enough to grab her, sure, but also, close enough that she could grab him. She hadn't realised it at first, but he wasn't staying out of her potential reach. He wasn't … afraid of her. And like he could feel her thinking all this, he said, "It won't get you anywhere."

Grace shook her head, innocent, like. *What?*

Weston smiled. "If you could overpower me, you'd be trapped down here, alone, without anyone to help." He stopped what he was doing and sat on the bed, next to her. Like a father figure. "Oh, yes, you could eat my decaying corpse, but then what? After that was gone?" He shook his head, rejected somehow, and took the tray with the empty plate and glass out, and around the corner without word.

Grace didn't speak either, somewhat bemused. Confused? *What a strange thing to say.*

Quite.

He left, but he didn't close the door. Then, a couple of minutes later he returned. With a bucket. He placed it on the floor to the side of the bed. Smiled at her.

Then he went and sat on the chair. In the darkness.

She stared at him for a second and then looked at

the bucket. Back to him.

"What?" he said. Voice even again.

Grace's stomach turned a little. She still needed to go, and he was going to fucking watch her, wasn't he? Grace got from the bed. The skirt he'd provided was long enough that at a squat it would provide a tent around the … proceedings. But Grace looked at the bucket and she felt sick. She might have felt better if she knew what he wanted. What he was getting from *this*? She stood over the bucket. Lined herself up. Dropped to squat, balancing herself on the edge of the bed with her arm.

Glancing to him, she could see nothing of his face. Just that he was there. Looking. Spying.

The piss didn't want to come out now. But she could feel the shit push against her anus. She looked away from him. At the wall. And breathed in slow. Turd pushing against her arse, crowning, and then the splop as it hit the dry bucket. Then another. A couple more. Little ones. As if the flood gates had opened.

The room filling with the rancid stench of shit, from her under-nourished and dehydrated body.

Then the piss wanted to come.

She relaxed her muscles, feeling the splashback of piss on her arse, as it bounced off the bottom of the bucket and the shit. She could smell that too. Without looking she knew it was going to be deep brown. She'd only had a glass or so of water in however long she'd been there. The initial gush slowed to a dribble and then stopped. She looked around. Not her first thought as it should have been, but she had nothing to wipe with. Fuck.

As if he knew, Weston stood, coming to her, pulling a fucking handkerchief from his pocket. "I apologise," he said. "I should have thought of that."

He passed it to her.

Reluctantly, Grace took it, sliding her hand under the skirt and wiping herself, carefully. She thought to hand it back to him, maybe it was what he wanted after all, but she dropped it into the bucket. She didn't want to be beaten if she was wrong. She stood after, carefully. She was at least clean now. For the first time in … however long. A quick look to Weston, then she retreated to the side of the bed. He hunched down and picked up the bucket without word. "How long have I been here?" she asked. Trying to sound normal, like this was some passing question to a waiter in a café.

"Does it matter?" he asked back. A question with a question. He looked surprised she'd asked.

Grace returned his question with a stare. Then asked, "Why am I here?"

Weston turned. Without further word he left. Grace sat on the edge of the bed, listening to him walk across the floor above.

And then the lights went out.

C H A P T E R   1 2

Plunged into perfect dark, Grace felt around on the bed, wrapped herself in the clean sheet that was there, and quickly found sleep. She wasn't looking for it, but the wear on her body was enough for her to slip into a blackness that mirrored the one that was there when she opened her eyes.

And they were both as terrifying as the other.

She jerked awake, unable to tell when her eyes were closed and when they weren't. How long had she been asleep? *Had* she been asleep? She tossed on the bed. Trying to face the direction of the room and not the wall. She could see nothing. Not even her hand inches from her eyes.

And time went by. She didn't know how much. She felt like hours had gone, when it could have been minutes, and not knowing when she slept, what were dreams, and what was real … until the lights came back on.

An hour? A day?

She could see better out of her eye now. That was something. But it suggested time had passed. She didn't need to use the bathroom again. But she was hungry. Was she hungry *again*, or *still* hungry? Weston had hardly given her enough food to sustain her, certainly not enough to fill her.

Just be glad that it wasn't shit, the voice suddenly said, returning after leaving her with her own thoughts for so long. The voice was right. At least it wasn't. She sat. Shivering. It was cold. Icy cold.

Probably night. She looked around quickly. There was no heater in there. No *heating*. She couldn't see if there was pipework on the far side of the room even with the light on.

Weston walked across the floor above. He was coming down.

She straightened herself. *Try to look innocent*, said the voice. *Harmless*.

She sat on the edge of the bed. Innocent. Harmless. She pushed her hair around. It was greasy. She could feel flecks of crust in it. Maybe dried blood. She smiled. Held it for a second, and then let it drop away. She pushed her arms down the side of her body, forward. It made her breasts protrude. Carol had said it was one way she could get what she wanted from her. They'd laughed, and Grace had used it—only in a joking way, of course—when she'd wanted Carol to get the popcorn if they were watching a film, or if she'd left her phone in the kitchen. She was thinking of using it now. To get Weston to do what she wanted. At least, to begin to. Crude. But if it worked. To this day, she had never tried to do it to anyone else. For all she knew it was something that Carol had just said.

To make her feel nice.

She shook the thoughts of her way. There was no need to think about a better place. Not while she was getting ready to play up to a man. This man.

The door opened. Footsteps.

Head up. Arms down. Breasts out.

Weston came around the corner. He barely gave her a second look. He was carrying the tray. He took the paper plate from the tray and placed it on the bed.

Grace turned with him, trying to get him to acknowledge her sexiness. Something to allude to the fact that he was at least interested. Anything.

He put the plate—bread, cheese—on the bed and quickly looked at her. Shook his head. Turned and walked to the corner. He stopped, head down. Looked like he was going to turn back and say something, but he didn't. He carried on walking. She heard the door remain open.

After he'd gone, she looked down at herself. She felt gross. And stupid. And not sexy. She wondered if she was ever going to feel that way again. She looked at the bread. Her appetite had gone now, too. Cold. Lonely. She picked it up though and tried it. Getting it in her mouth was like opening the flood gates. The taste made her crave more, and before she knew it, it was gone.

Almost as soon as she had finished, Weston returned to the room. Turned the corner, picked up the plate and retreated to the darkness on the other side of the room. "How are you feeling?" he asked.

It was a sudden show of humanity, taking Grace back slightly. She tried to look demure. "It's cold down here," she said. "Can I go upstairs? To where you are? It must be warmer. Up there." She sounded stupid. She knew she did. There was no way he was going to fall for it, of course, but she had to try.

"Do you think I'm deranged?"

She did. *Yes*. He had her trapped in his basement, locked up like some fucking animal. Of course she thought he was deranged. "No, of course not." She smiled. Hoped it came off as sincere. "I like it when you come down and spend time with me." The words made her feel sick. Felt like she had shit in her mouth again.

"I'm not *trying* to hurt you," he said. He spoke quietly. There was a hesitation in there that Grace saw as a good sign. Maybe he wasn't all bad?

"I know that," she said. "We're … friends, right?" He was in the darkness, and she couldn't see his response, if he nodded. "So, you can tell me why I'm here, right?" She knew she was pushing her luck.

"Don't talk to me like I'm a fucking simpleton," he snapped. From the darkness.

Grace withdrew onto the bed slightly. Fear gripped her. She'd pushed him too far, and he was pissed. "No, I—"

The chair clattered, grinding on the floor as he stood. Angry. He strode straight to the corner and around without stopping. He didn't even look at her.

"No, wait, Weston, I …" But he was gone. He didn't shut the door. She heard him stomping on a set of stairs for the first time. It sounded like the door around the corner led straight to a set of stairs and up. It confirmed her basement theory. Regardless, she felt like she'd just taken one step forward and two steps back.

He went across the room above.

Silence for a moment.

Then he started back.

CHAPTER 13

Weston returned to the corner. He stood there, half around the corner, and half not. Grace stared at him for a second. She'd already tensed tightly, expecting him to return solely to beat her. "I didn't mean to," she said.

"Didn't mean to *what*?" Menacing. Angry. She'd touched something. When they were talking. He'd lost control. *That* was why he had left.

She was sure of it.

"I … I don't know," she replied quietly. She knew it was the wrong thing to say. He wasn't going to be happy with the wrong answer.

"Fucking hell." He hissed the words out. Barely escaping through his lips, whistling through his teeth.

"Sorry." It was her turn to barely get the words out that time. They released as more of a resignation than an actual apology. She was apologising to herself for fucking up, maybe? Maybe the voice said it.

"I just …" Weston began. "I just …" He was breathing hard. High pitching singing coming from his nose as he huffed in and out. He looked at her. "Why won't you …" He stopped, looking for the words. "… behave?"

Then he came at her.

Grace tried to get back, across the bed, like the wall on the other side of it might offer some protection. He grabbed her, spry and strong for a man of his age. Fuck it. He probably wasn't *that* old. It was just the perception of the grey hair and lines on his face. The ones there when he smiled, and now, when he was angry. He grabbed her foot as she tried to pull it back, under herself, and dragged her across the bed to the front, to where he was. "Bitch," he mumbled. "Needs a fucking lesson." He punched her. The blow landed in her side. On her ribs. She felt the vibrations of it roll across her skeleton, slosh her insides about. It paralysed her long enough that he could pull the sheet she'd gathered in her panic away from her. Take one wrist in his hand and pull that away too. He grabbed at her t-shirt. She thought he was going to pull her clothes off, but she hadn't realised that he was going to *tear* them from her.

He grabbed the shirt by the neck and yanked it. Hard as he could, tearing the fabric away from her, revealing her body underneath, bare. Bruised. She was helpless, prone, frozen by the suddenness of the attack. He ripped the shirt from her and as it pulled, it scarred her skin, red with welts as he drew it hard over her flesh.

She screamed out, but he didn't stop. Didn't break for breath. He just pulled the shirt—now a rag—from her and tossed it over his shoulder to the darkness on the other side of the room. Grace tried to stop him, nothing more than flails really. She wasn't a fighter. She could only get her hand in the way. The one he wasn't holding. She pled. "Please ..." she cried, "... don't." She knew where this was going.

Weston slipped his fingers into the waist of the skirt next. Did the same with that, too. Hauling the clothing from her. No words. Just rough, violent actions. Leaving her naked on the bed. Still holding her. She'd given up trying to stop him. He was far too strong. She wasn't pathetic, or useless, but he was quick.

He punched her again. Same place. Knocking all the fight, the air, the … everything … from her, and she flopped, as if she'd lost consciousness. Let him do as he would, then. She couldn't stop him.

He was breathing hard.

She could smell him. His sweat. Stink of rotten flesh that untended body odour was. "Please," she said again. One last try, pain like she was being crushed inside her torso.

He had stopped. He was staring at her.

Grace shuddered in horror. Pain. Cold. She was naked under his eye, and for the first time she could see the wont in his look. He was leering over her. Taking in the sight of her flesh, bare, but not moving. She couldn't help it, but she glanced to his groin. To his cock, proud in his trousers.

He was hard. For her. To fuck her.

Rape her.

She lifted her free arm and covered her eyes. She didn't want to see what he was going to do next. She didn't want to witness him. See him.

Then he let her arm go.

Grace didn't move, blinded by her arm. She lay, crumpled on the bed, and waited for him to do what he was going to. Waited. There was some movement, only a little, and then the room fell silent. She expected him to be standing there. About to leap on her again. Fuck her. So still, she didn't move.

Eventually, she lifted her arm from her face. Shivering in the cold.

He was gone. The sheet was gone from the bed. Her clothes—rags—taken from the shadows on the floor on the other side of the room. Grace looked around, pulling her knees up to her chest, wrapping her arms around herself. He'd left her in the cold with

nothing. To freeze.
     Punishment.

CHAPTER 14

Grace lay on the bed. The lights went out hours ago. She was sore, but that didn't matter. She was dehydrated, which was a problem. But she was cold. So cold. It must have been something like four, maybe five degrees? Naked. She knew she'd slept— well, lost consciousness—at some point, because she'd awoken covered in sweat. The cold penetrating every inch of her.

She guessed she was sick. A fever. Maybe? Maybe just nightmares.

"Hello?" she called out. "Weston?" She waited for a minute. To see if he was going to move across the ceiling. When nothing happened, she shouted, "Please. I didn't mean to. Please."

And then she waited for what felt like more hours. Perhaps it was.

Maybe he couldn't hear her. Maybe he'd left the house and she was alone. He'd left her there to die. Disappointed in her, for what, she had no idea. She pulled herself from the bed and started to move about in the dark. Tried to get warm. Move blood around in her body. She needed to pee. Her bones ached from the cold. Joints sore. She ran her hands over her skin to try and make heat, but her skin hurt. She could feel physical sores appearing. Lack of food? No movement? She had no idea. The metal clasp around her foot had chaffed the fuck out of the skin there, she could feel that much.

And she now had no idea how long she had been there.

Two days? Three?

Her mind awash—how many times had she eaten? Twice? Bread, twice. The first time … she stopped thinking about it, unwilling to puke again at the thought. She'd only been to the bathroom once. That she remembered. He brought a bucket. It must have been three days at least. Why had no one come for her?

"Weston?" she called into the darkness. Then, weakly, she continued, "Please … I'll do anything you say."

The lights flickered on, and Grace raised her hand to protect her eyes from the light. Not bright, but after the perfect dark, stinging. Harsh.

He came across the ceiling. The footsteps.

Grace waited. She hurt. Shivering. Resigned.

The door. Then he was at the corner of the room. He looked at her. "What?" he asked. "What will you do?"

Had … had he heard her? She tried to smile. "Anything you want," she said. "Please, I'm cold. I need something to eat. I'll do anything." She just repeated it. She didn't know what he wanted. Something that yesterday she would have guessed at, but it didn't seem like he wanted her. Not biblically. So what did he want?

He sighed. Staring at her. He looked pitifully at her. Like he felt sorry for her. She could feel the tears welling. She didn't want to give up, but her body had. And the voice in her head. The one that seemed so full of vigour … even that seemed to have abandoned her. She'd been down there long enough that she felt like everyone had abandoned her. She looked up at him, through the tears. He was nodding.

"Yes," he said. "Anything."

She returned the nod. Anything to get him to give her something. Warmth. Food.

"Will you fuck me?"

Fuck? *Fuck.* Grace nodded. "Yes," she said weakly. She knew it. *Knew it.* This was what it was about all along. Fucking. He already had his hand on his belt buckle. But he'd stopped. Paused. Thinking about it.

She could see he was getting hard in his trousers. Dirty cunt. Grace opened her legs. She looked down at herself quickly. She was dirty from having no clothes. She felt thinner from having so little food. She was shaking all over. Cold? Fear? Then he unbuckled his belt. He walked closer to her. Got close enough that she could smell him. Fucker even smelt good. He smelt like he was doused in some aftershave. She wished he *was* smelly. Something else she could hate him for.

Like he was trying to make this *nice*.

He opened the belt. Then his trousers. His cock was hidden under a pair of shorts. He pushed his trousers over his arse. Then pulled his shorts to the side. Cock out through the leg hole. Very romantic. "Suck it," he said. "If you think about hurting me, I'll beat you half to death, and then leave you here to die of starvation."

Grace nodded. She was looking at his penis. Erect. Staring at it. It wasn't the first time she'd given a man a blow job. Been a while though. She was sure she could remember how. It didn't smell. She was only inches from it, and she couldn't smell it. That was something. The last time she'd had cock in her mouth was at Uni. Some of those boys weren't as clean as Weston.

That was something, she kept saying to herself.

Over. And Over.

He shuffled forward, like an impetuous boy. Impatient.

Grace leant forward, pursing her lips to an O and sliding them over his head, the shaft. It was an average sized cock, she supposed. Glad she didn't have to deep throat or anything. *That was something.* Her mouth was dry. Lips chaffed. Her tongue felt sandy. But Weston didn't seem to care. Thankfully.

She slid up and down, best as she could remember, Weston grunting out some satisfaction. Grace reached around behind him and brought her hands up to his thighs. She pulled him in, closer. Made it look like she wanted to please him. Pleasure him. But she was feeling. Anything in his pockets? The keys to the fucking chain on her leg. A weapon. At this point, she was ready to kill him, and eat him. If it meant staying alive. She thought about biting his cock off. She'd read about that in some shitty book once—but she was doubtful she could bite the whole thing off before he could stove her head in with his fists.

So she pleasured him. Feeling around.

He was grunting harder. He'd gotten to the point of coming quickly. Probably hadn't had any in a while. Fucker. He was going to jizz in her mouth. She didn't want that, but this was something she was doing *willingly* … so he thought. She needed to ensure she didn't retch. He was grinding himself now. Fucking her mouth. She was trying to keep her teeth back. Didn't want to get punched in the head. While she worked his pockets.

Nothing.

He had *literally* nothing on him.

Then he jerked. Came in her mouth. Hot, sticky

jizz coating the roof of her mouth, pushing itself, firing, into the back of her throat. Making her want to cough. She swallowed to stop herself from choking, nothing more than instinct, sucking his cum down her throat. She could feel it, phlegm thick, trailing down her like a slug. Towards her gut. Turning her stomach. She concentrated on not puking.

Then he was shuddering.

"Enough," he barked, backing away quickly. It was his turn to shake now. He looked flustered. "Yes. Enough," he said more quietly, quickly pushing his cock back into his shorts, pulling his trousers up. "Good," he said. "You're getting there."

Grace wiped her mouth with the back of her forearm. Realising she still had her legs open, she closed them. "Please," she said. "Please can I have something in return?"

Weston rung his hands together, like they were cold. Like he had the fucking cheek to get cold—then he turned, without word. Around the corner.

Gone.

CHAPTER 15

Grace sat there, unmoving. Stunned. Stunned that he'd left like that. She was sure that he was going to give her something in return. *In return for compliance.* She looked up at the dark ceiling as he walked across the floor above. And he didn't have anything in his pockets. Could be that he didn't usually carry anything, could be that he was actually careful. Whatever.

Maybe she was going to have to kill him, and think about the ramifications later.

Then he walked back across. He was coming back. Bringing her something. She waited. He came to the door, to the corner of the room. He had something behind his back. Food. She was hoping it was food. He stepped over to her, still sitting on the edge of the bed. Like a good little girl. Daddy's little whore.

He stood. Close to her. Showed her.

He had a roll of tape. Duct tape looking stuff. Grace frowned. He picked at the tape for a second, trying to find the end of it, and when he did, he pinched it, and pulled it. It made that growl that packing tape makes when you pulled a foot of it from the reel. *Wwwweeeeeeerrrrrppppp.* He showed it to her. Seemed proud of it. Then he pushed himself onto her. The tape over her eyes. And around circling her head with it. Around and around mummifying her. Blinded, she flailed out. Kicking as best she could with the chain attached. Punching as the tape went around her head, sticking her hair to her head, over her nose. If he covered her mouth she wasn't going to be able to breath. The sound of the tape getting duller as it covered her ears. Deafening her to hear nothing but the faintest of sound.

The voice in her head said, *this is it then*.

Then it went quiet.

Pain suddenly began to shudder through her body. Ribs. Back. Chest. He must be punching her or kicking her. She couldn't tell. The tape never went over her mouth though. She tried screaming. Calling out. *Help. Stop.* She stopped fighting when he beat the last of the battle from her. Pain like that first time he beat her rolling across her like the tide coming in. Stabbing at her. She could feel the burning in her bones. Her torso, arms and legs, and the tightness of the tape wrapped her head and face.

Why?

Then a sudden calm. He must have moved away. The room in silence, her hearing dulled to nearly nothing. Blind. She lay there. She was crying, the tears slipping around in the tiniest of space where the tape didn't meet her skin, in the concave of her eye sockets. "Please," she said. Without the use of her ears, it sounded bass in tone. "Why?" Then, "What did I do?" She could have been talking to herself though. He might not have even been in the room.

She lay there. On the bed. She could feel the mattress below her.

Then there were hands on her. He was moving her. Manoeuvring her into a position. On the bed. Over it. The crack on her bones as her knees hit the solid floor. Pain shooting up her legs. His weight on her back, pushing her torso into the mattress.

Then he was inside her.

Fucking her. Raping her.

She tried screaming out. Weakly. Crying. She knew she should fight back, but she could barely breathe. She had no senses left. So cold she couldn't feel. Anything. Apart from him. Inside. Jamming his cunt cock inside her. Pulling at her. She could feel the skin inside her, sharp sudden belts of pain. Tearing. Bleeding.

She felt him, jerking as he came.

Then nothing. Gone. He'd left her. Left her there, half on the bed, half off. She waited. Didn't move. Part of her wanted to move. Part of her wanted to die. She just wanted it over. Now it had gotten to this. Where she was sure it was going to go in the end. Grace pulled herself up, onto the bed, and curled, foetal. She lay, breathing in and out through her mouth. Sounded like she was scuba diving in her head, the dominant sound. The *only* sound.

Please, she thought. End it.

No, said the voice.

C H A P T E R   1 6

Hours gone by. Maybe. It was impossible to tell. Grace had no idea. She was so cold she could barely feel anything. She'd tried picking at the tape some time ago. But she could barely feel her fingers. Fingertips hurt. She wondered if it was cold enough that she would get frostbite. She couldn't see to tell.

Her body hurt from the beating that Weston had given her. She had felt down between her legs. After. There was wet coming from her. Could have been cum. Could have been blood. No way of knowing. So she lay there. Waiting to see if Weston was going to come back and rape her again before she died.

No water in what … two days? Her memory was a fog. Time was an unfathomable creature at this point. No way of telling night from day, even before he'd taken her eyes from her.

She felt him … his presence. He was there in the room. Watching her. She hadn't heard him come in. Maybe he'd been there for some time. "Hello?" The word croaked out of her. Last thing she'd had in her throat was his cum. Not exactly good lube.

"It's me," Weston said.

The sound of his voice—dulled as it was—made her jump like a shitty horror movie. It was louder than she expected, silence filling the room for so long.

"Are you okay?"

What a fucking cunt. "No," she said. "Cold."

"I know. I'm going to cut the tape from you now, okay?"

He hadn't waited for her to answer him. She felt

him come up next to her. She could feel something on her skin. His clothes brushing against her most likely, but it felt strange. She could barely feel anything, her skin itself, numbed by the cold. He touched her. She pulled away.

"There, there," he said. Like she was some dumb animal caught on some barbed wire.

She felt the tape move. He was pushing something about there. Sliding something between her and the tape. A blade … no … scissors? She felt the tape loosen. He wasn't touching her anywhere else, he just appeared to be leaning over her, judging by the feel of his clothing on her. Teasing the tape back. Cutting it away. A little at a time.

Snip. Pull. She could feel the tape being drawn back, dragging on her skin. Inflaming it as the taut glue yanked on her.

Eventually, he gently slipped the blades of the scissors into the tape that covered her eye. She fought the initial reaction—to lurch backwards, as this point of metal was suddenly in the gap between the tape and her eyeball, but she stopped herself. She waited until he'd pulled the scissors back out, he slipped his finger under the edge of the tape, pulling it away from her, and she could feel his knuckle, the last one on his forefinger, pushing gently against her eyeball, her eye shut. Like she was at the doctor's office, undergoing some random shitty procedure. She felt her skin stretch on the side of her eye as the piece of tape was torn off. Another piece of the puzzle, removed.

The tape was tight on her hair.

She opened her eyes. Could finally see out of the one. The one he'd just untaped. Bright light. Burning. She looked up at him, stood over her like a fucking dentist. He had a pair of long nosed scissors in his hand. Finger in one hole, thumb in the other. Close to her. Looking down on her.

He smiled. *Fucking* smiled. "Getting there," he said. "Don't move."

Grace saw the blade of the scissors slide into the tape over her other eye. Snip. Pull. He worked slowly, methodically. He seemed to be trying not to hurt her. Grace closed her eyes. She didn't want to look at him that close. She could smell his breath. Vile, old tea. Occasionally he would sniff. The sound bouncing around in her deadened ears. Until he finished working on the second eye.

He stepped back. "Open up," he said.

Grace did. She could still see the bits of tape like all he'd done is cut eye holes in her face-tape mask. She looked at him. He was trying to smile. Maybe … trying not to laugh. He was standing between her and the light, and it was hard to tell, with most of his face in shadow. She looked at the scissors. She wanted them. She wanted to throw herself at him and take them. She thought she could, too, if she had wanted to. But the voice said, *no, you're chained to the bed, remember?*

And that stopped her. She could take them and plunge them into his eye. Take his sight. Stick them in. Out. In. Out. Shake it all about. She smiled to herself, then coughed, covering it.

Weston must have seen what she was looking at, because the scissors went down in his hand, around behind his back. He cleared his throat. "Yes, anyway." He was looking at her naked body. Watching her suffer. Shiver. Trodden down. Weak. *Or so he thought.* "I think you're coming along."

Whatever that meant.

Then he left. Out. The door remained open. Grace

heard. Then he was above her. Across. She felt the tape still stuck to her face. She clawed weakly at it. It covered most of her face. Around her head, she could feel it tangled still, stuck in her hair.

A few minutes later, he was coming back. Across the floor above.

Grace stopped, and let her hands drop to her sides. She looked down at herself. Lowly. That was how she felt. Her nipples were hard. Pink and hard in a sea of goose bumps, purple and black, blotched with bruising. He came back to the corner and tossed a nightshirt to the bed next to her. A blanket.

She touched it. Resting her hand weakly on it. Better than a sheet. Warmer. She looked back to him, standing there like he was waiting for her thank him. She flashed him a little smile and pulled the nightshirt over her head. It wasn't more than an over sized t-shirt, really. Then she pulled the blanket out, unfolding it until it was big enough for her to crawl under.

She listened to him leave. Vague, dull footsteps.

The door closed.

The lights went out.

In the darkness, Grace picked at the tape that covered her ears, as the warmth returned to her body … as did the pain.

CHAPTER 17

Grace was awoken by the sound of Weston coming in. She looked out from the warmth of the blanket and over to the corner. She had managed to unpick some of the tape from her ears. She could hear now, but attempting to pull the tape from her hair was fruitless. It just pulled like bubble gum. Painful. Yanking at the roots.

Weston stood at the corner. Tray. Something on the tray. A cup. "Here," he said. "I thought you might like a nice cup of tea."

What. The. Fuck.

Grace stared at him trying to process the information. A nice cup of tea? *A nice cup of tea.* Huh. Fuck. Fucker. She pulled the blanket tight around her. Sat. She kept her body from his line of sight. She made sure he couldn't see the nightshirt he'd provided. Probably getting off on it. He was standing there, looking a little uncomfortable.

"It'll warm your cockles," he said.

Like an old man. Grandfatherly. Grace tried to smile, and failed. She wanted to lull him into … something. She just didn't want to piss him off, she supposed. Didn't want a beating. The tape. To be raped. *Not again.* He stepped forward, holding the tray out for her to take the tea.

The steam rose from the cup furiously in the cold of the room.

Grace slipped her hand out from the blanket and took the cup. The chill nipping at her flesh, warmed properly for the first time in days. It felt like longer.

Perhaps it was? She held the cup. Noticed she was shaking. Also noticed that Weston was staring. He was looking between her and the cup. Expectant.

She remembered what he had said. Before. When she first woke up, maybe. He said something like, "If you'd just drunk the tea …" *Something like that*. She had assumed that he meant if she'd just drank the tea, then maybe she'd have just been fine. But what if … what if it was drugged. Maybe he just meant that if she'd just drank the tea, he wouldn't have had to hit her with the tray? Her eyes dropped to the tea, and it was her turn to look at it. What if it was drugged now? Why else would he have suddenly brought her tea?

He seemed to be nodding slightly.

That was it, wasn't it? *It was drugged.* She raised the cup to her lips and tipped the liquid forward, pushing it against her lips, but not taking it into her mouth. Faking drinking the tea. She lowered the cup. Smiled. Tried not to inhale the steam. Poisoned steam. She looked at him over the rim of the cup. Now he was nodding like a fucking dog.

Yes, the voice said. *That's it. Let him think you're doing as he wants.*

She did it again. The fake drink. She lowered her eyes so they were only open a crack, then flicked them open like she was trying not to fall asleep. All the while watching him. Judging him on his reaction.

Was he expecting her to fall asleep?

He seemed to be. His excitement was rising as she was drinking the liquid. She looked at the cup. A poisoned chalice. Lolled her head a little from side to side. Hoping this was what it was supposed to look like. "So tired," she mumbled. A glance to Weston. Nodding. Grinning. He was going for it. "Barely keep my eyes open," she said. She offered the cup forward, back to Weston. He took it. Didn't seem to have any idea that it still had the same amount of liquid in it that it had before.

That's it, the voice said.

She lolloped to the side, slumping down on to the mattress, and pulling the blanket in, like she was being dragged willingly into the slumber. Then she waited.

A couple of minutes went by. She heard Weston put the cup down on the side table. Then he touched her shoulder. She stopped herself from flinching.

He must be going to move you. Why else would he need you out?

Yes.

There was a noise. A jangle. Keys. He had *keys*. Then she felt him kneel down, pushing against her slightly. He was messing with her foot. Her ankle. Undoing the clasp. She heard it clank to the floor, the cold burn of the metal, released from her. She opened her eyes a crack. He was there. At her feet. He wasn't paying her enough attention to know that she was awake. A glance around. She sat, fast as she could, throwing the blanket from her. Knee up, into his face. She contacted with Weston, his nose splitting open on contact, blood spurting out and down, and flicking up, all at once. He made a dull grunting sound. Head snapped back. He froze like that for a second. Grace stood, wavering, weak, her feet cold on the floor. She picked up the cup from the side and swung it. Hard as she could into Weston's skull. His temple. He grunted again as the thin skin of the side of his head cracked open as the cup shattered, the china grinding into his flesh, jagged on the bone.

Grace looked at what she had left in her had as

Weston reached up, cradling his face, blood oozing out between his fingers. She still had half the cup, brought down to a jagged knife-edge, the rest of it scattered across the floor. She brought the cup up like a dagger, and thrust it as hard as she could, down, into the top of Weston's leg.

Instinct said to stab him through the heart.

But the voice said *no*.

Break him. Break him like he was trying to do to you.

He screamed out in agony, his hands, plastered in blood, left his face and went to his leg. Half a cup jutting out the trousers. Sticking in the flesh. She looked around the floor, quickly. The clasp. Still had the key sticking out of it. Discarded to the floor. The chain still attached. She slapped the clasp around his ankle, locking it shut while he was taken with the concern over his leg. Pulled the key out, grasping it tightly in her hand. Then she stood. Punched him in his bloody face, pathetic and crying. Weak. Disoriented. She stooped down and pulled the half cup from his leg, and then retreated to the darkness on the other side of the room. Blood slicked out the leg wound, as he hunched over it, crying out in pain, the blood from his face dropping onto it. "Please," he said. "Jesus Christ."

Fucker, said the voice.

Grace sat in the chair, breathing hard. Waiting. She watched him flail about. Not even realising he was trapped there. She was out. She rested for only seconds. Stood. Hurried to the door around the corner. A flight of stairs. Up. She *was* in the basement. Leaving the door open, she went upstairs.

Freedom, the voice said.

CHAPTER 18

Grace reached the top of the stairs. A little light headed. She fumbled the door. Open. The light out there bright. Daytime. She had no idea how many days she'd missed. A look down at herself. She was … surprised? Amazed? She could still hear Weston in the basement. He was screaming for her to go back and help him.

She blinked away the sun, the bright, looking around.

The house looked different to what she remembered. It was ornate, wasn't it? Expensive. This place looked barely decorated. She hadn't spent long in the house, maybe she was disoriented. She squinted around the room. A window to the side, a door. Grace went to the door, leading further into the house. She didn't want to go further into the house, she wanted to leave, of course. She wanted to get out. Freedom, as the voice had said. But into the house she had to go.

Opening the door into a hallway, Grace looked out. The house … it was different. The hallway led down the side of a set of stairs. She walked along it slowly, her hand on the wall, guiding her. She could see the front door at the end of the stairs.

It wasn't the same front door as before. It wasn't … the same …

She started to hurry, the pain in her torso stabbing at her, her legs barely able to hold up her weight. She ran to the front door. Looked through the glass.

She wasn't in the same house. She'd been taken

somewhere else. After she'd been …. She reached out and grabbed the door handle, twisting it back and forth. She wanted to scream but the noise came out like a pissed off bovine. Her face contorted into fear, sadness … *where was she?* She was sure, so sure, that this was it. The door locked, Grace spapped her hands on the glass, screaming for help, frustration taking over rational thought.

Then a noise came from behind her.

Nothing more than a creak. Someone there. She turned, breath held. Expecting Weston to be standing there, she came face to face with someone else. A glimmer of recognition there. She … knew him from somewhere. He was frowning. Confused. He looked more than a little annoyed.

Clearly, not an innocent bystander. But it didn't stop the single word, "Please," from falling from Grace's mouth. Tears streaming down her face. Over the remnants of the tape.

"The fuck," the man whispered. "How the hell did you get up here?"

The tears came harder for Grace. *So close.*

The man came forward, striding to her, bringing up a hand, a fist. She should have run, but the fight wasn't there. It had been stolen from her. Right there. He punched her. Hard. Her head snapped backwards and slammed against the glass in the front door. She heard a weak grunt come from somewhere within her, then she was sliding. Back on the door. Down.

The man grabbed her, pulling her back up and dragging her across the floor. Across tiled flooring. She knew she'd seen it before somewhere, her thoughts spinning as her brain rattled from the blow. She glanced to the side. A mirror. Wall hung. She could see the man in profile, dragging her as he walked backwards, his hands under her arms, pulling.

She had tape strung around her head. She could see the sides of her legs, bruised, and beaten. She looked up to the man's face. Then she remembered him. He was the man next door. The one who worked nights.

Was that where she was?

She could feel a blackness trying to take her. Grooming her consciousness for sleep. She tried to blink it away.

He's taking you back, the voice said.

If she went back. If she allowed it, she would die. She knew that. Weston was bleeding badly. They wouldn't give her a second chance. Either today, or tomorrow, or months from now, she *would* die.

He backed into the door, and pushed it open, jiggling it around with his feet, holding her up, thinking she was unconscious.

She was still vague. Broken, both physically and mentally. Weston's voice rang out from the basement. And this one, he dragged her across the room to the basement door. He went in first. Pulling her, as he backed down the stairs.

Now, said the voice.

He'd dragged her until her feet dropped from the first step to the second. She raised her knees, and braced her feet on the stairs, and pushed.

Pushed them both backwards down the stairs into the darkness.

CHAPTER 19

"What's going on? Where are you?" Weston's voice was weak. Pathetic. The maggot was whining. Grace listened to him as she lay there. It felt like her head was full of blood, sloshing around like a boat taking on water. She hadn't braved the movement of her limbs yet. *Great idea*, the voice said, *great idea*. She could tell that *he* wasn't moving either. Whatever his name was. She could feel him. Half underneath her.

She opened her eyes. Stared into the black of the ceiling. She moved to look, a burning throb blasted from her head, and she rested it back, having seen nothing but the light coming from the top of the stairs.

She was alive. *That was something.*

Grace tried to put thoughts into order. Pigeon holing things to get them straight. Currently they all seemed scattered like she'd dropped them when they fell down the stairs. She moved her toes. Wiggled them. Hurt, but they moved. Same with her fingers. Okay. No broken spine. She *thought*.

Lifting her head again, Grace looked to the side. Shrouded in the shadows was the other one. The man that was dragging her. She couldn't tell if he was breathing or not. She had to move. If he was alive he could move at any moment.

"Hello?" Weston called. "Help me."

Grace lifted her head again. She let out a short cry, alerting Weston to her presence.

"You?" he said. Quieter. "Please," he said.

She rolled over, pain spiking in every corner of

every inch of her. Her *skin* hurt. She looked at the man on the floor. His elbow bone—whatever it was— was sticking from the joint, spearing through the skin like a javelin. She leant over a little further. His face was one big gash, blood smeared, with a crevice down it like the Grand Canyon. His neck twisted at a ludicrous angle, another bone sticking wildly out of that. Grace pulled her head back. Disgusted by the sight.

She got to her knees and pulled herself up the wall, wobbly, to her feet.

"Grace," Weston said quietly. "Please. It wasn't me that …" He went quiet for a moment. "I didn't have sex with you. That was Justin." He spoke, his voice monotone. "My son. Is he there?"

Grace went to the corner, leaning her weight against the wall. "He's dead," she said. Weston was sitting on the floor, one hand over his leg wound, and a pool of blood beneath him. It looked like the main gush of the blood had slowed. He was looking down, a spindle of blood strung from his face down to between his legs.

When he looked up, his face had stopped bleeding, but he was a pulpy mess. He nodded. "Call the police," he said. Resigned.

Grace stared at him. She moved over to the chair in the shadows and sat, watching him.

Weston sat there for a few moments, before looking at her again. She knew he couldn't see much more than her outline, her silhouette, as she had, his. "Well? What are you waiting for?" he said.

The voice said, *fuck him*.

Grace nodded. She stood. "Maybe later," she said. Leaving the room, she stepped over Justin, and returned to the top floor. She went to the windows and looked out. She could see the street from there. It was the first house on the street. The one she had seen him in. Before going next door. To the house that most certainly didn't belong to Weston.

She could hear him call out, dull. Between the closed door and the floorboards, you could quite easily forget he was there.

Going upstairs, Grace found clothes. Women's clothes. Some were hers, washed and put away in a wardrobe in a back bedroom, others belonged to other girls. She guessed that she wasn't the first visitor that had stayed there.

She pulled on a skirt tucking her over sized night shirt into it, and pulled on a pair of trainers that fit.

Went back downstairs to the kitchen.

Made herself a cup of coffee, before returning to the basement. She hurt. All over, but a calm had taken her like the ocean. She went to Weston, and sat, her coffee in her hand.

"Called them?" he asked. Not really a question. An assumption.

"Tell me what you were doing in that house? The painting. The one above the fireplace."

"What does it matter now? I've lived next door to fucking Gerald McAllister for over a decade. Got fed up with him, and his highfalutin ideas about the street. Body is in his basement. Then you showed up. I knew my son would like you." He gestured around the basement. "He likes the girls."

"Liked," she corrected. "Dead remember?"

The pain was clear in Weston's face. "I remember. I saw you coming from the window, and knew I had to get you in the house. So I pulled the painting down. Knew that someone with smarts would suss that I wasn't the cunt in the picture. When are they coming?"

"Who?"

"The police."

Grace took a sip of her coffee. She wasn't cold anymore. But numb. She got up and stepped over to the side table, putting the coffee down. Went to the corner. "Who said I've called them?" She went to Justin and rolled him over. Over and over.

Until he reached the corner of the room. Weston looked away. He was a pale, shadow of the man he was not an hour ago. Then she rolled Justin closer still. Until Weston had the younger man within his reach.

"Pretty well sound proofed down here," Grace said. "I guess … I guess I should be going."

"What?" Weston said, nothing more than a whisper.

"I should be going. I've left you a drink." She waved to the coffee. Then she kicked the corpse. "Something to eat."

"No," Weston said. "You can't. You've called the police, right?" He started to scrabble about, pulling on the chain, clasped to his foot.

"You'll be fine."

Three weeks later, Grace crossed the end the street, sitting on the bus, on the way to her hospital appointment. After she'd left the house she went to the local hospital, claiming to have no memory of the events of the previous days. No idea where she'd been. With who. Vengeance seemed sweeter than justice, somehow.

And she wondered …

… if Weston was still alive down there, eating his

way through the corpse of his son. Hoping to be discovered before he ran out of food.

About the Author

Ash is a British horror author. He resides in the south, in the Garden of England. He writes horror that is sometimes fantastical, sometimes grounded, but always deeply graphic, and black with humour.

Printed in Great Britain
by Amazon